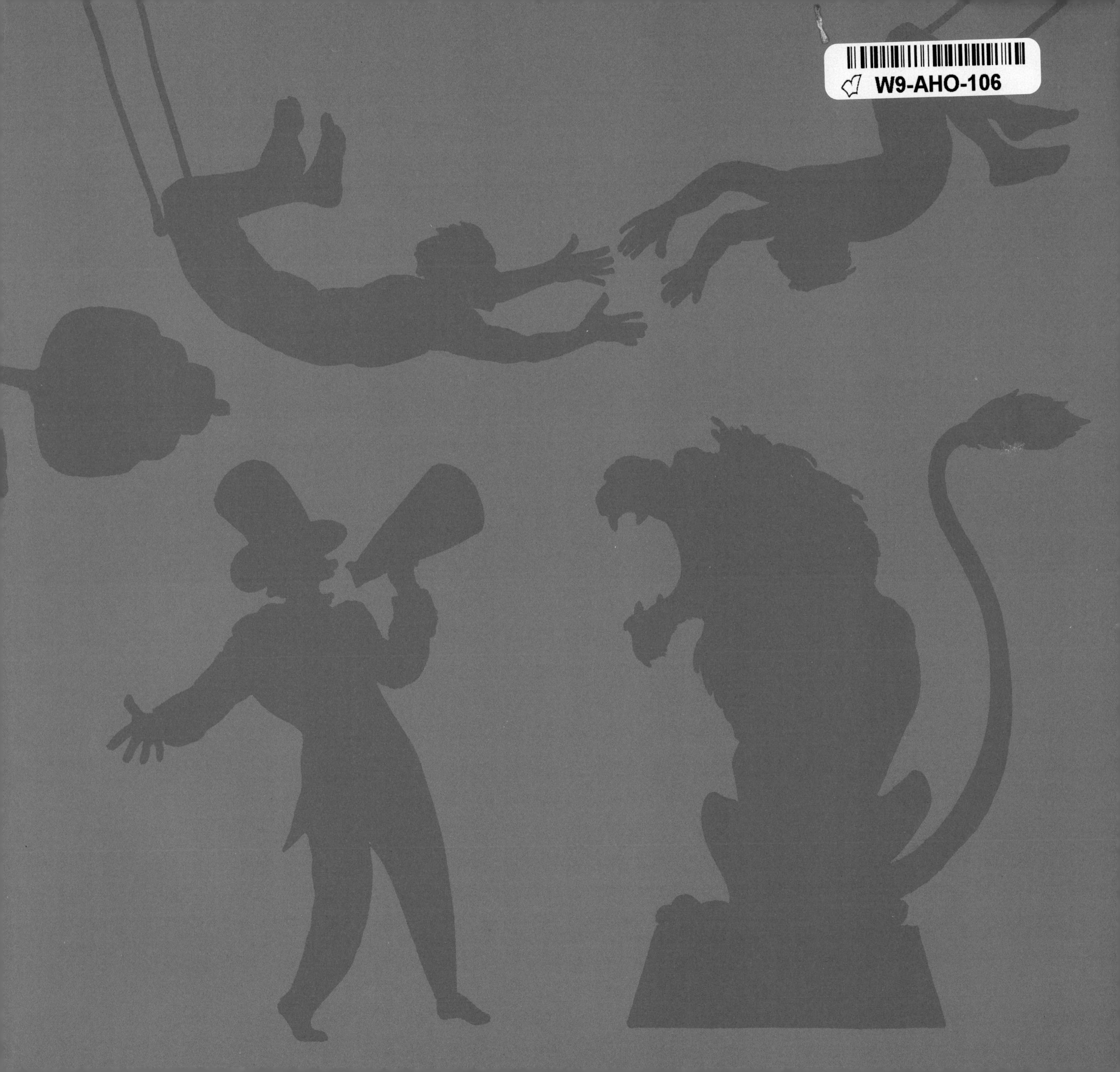

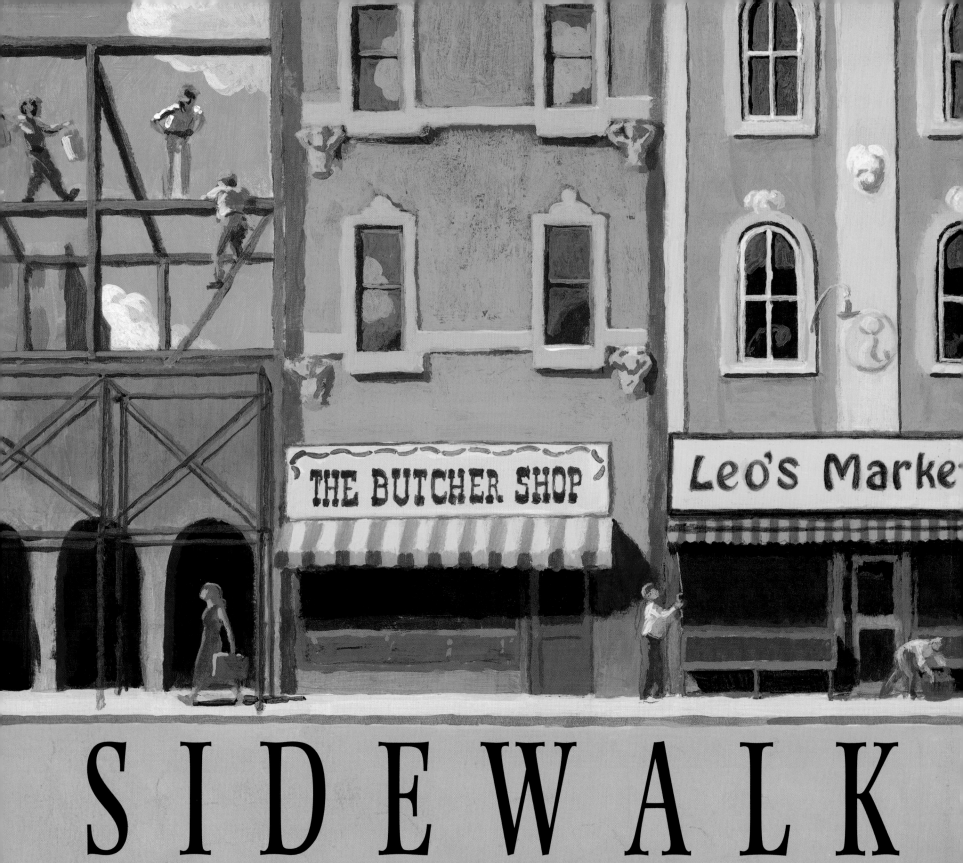

SIDEWALK

presented by **Paul Fleischman** and **Kevin Hawkes**

COMING SOON... WORLD-RENOWNED
...GARIBALDI CIRCUS!!!! . . . .

CIRCUS

CANDLEWICK PRESS
CAMBRIDGE, MASSACHUSETTS

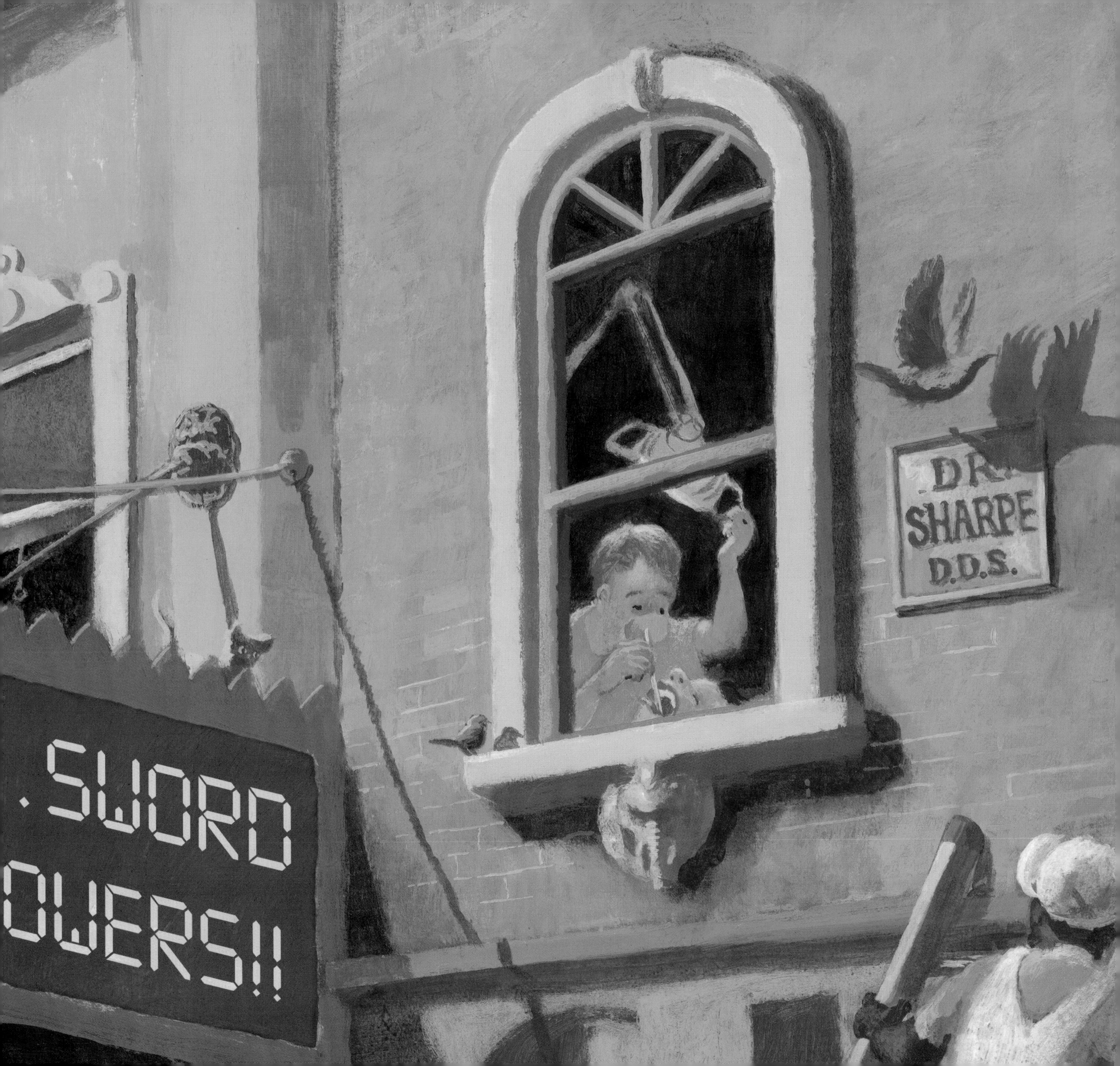
DR.
SHARPE
D.D.S.
. SWORD
OWERS!!

SEE THE BORO
. . . THE FLYING

VSKY BROTHERS ON . . . .
TRAPEZE!!!!!! . . . .

COMING SOON . . . WORLD-RENOWNED . . . GARIBALDI CIRCUS!!!!!!!! . . . . . .

GREAT TEBALDI
PRINCE OF TIGHTR

To Ann Stott—K. H.

Story and text copyright © 2004 by Paul Fleischman
Illustrations copyright © 2004 by Kevin Hawkes

First edition 2004

Library of Congress Cataloging-in-Publication Data

Fleischman, Paul.
Sidewalk circus / Paul Fleischman ; illustrated by Kevin Hawkes.—1st ed.
p.   cm.
Summary: A young girl watches as the activities across the street from her bus stop
become a circus.
ISBN 0-7636-1107-7
[1. City and town life—Fiction. 2. Circus—Fiction. 3. Stories without words.]
I. Hawkes, Kevin, ill. II. Title.
PZ7.F59918 Si 2003
[E]—dc21   2002074168

2 4 6 8 10 9 7 5 3 1

Printed in China

The illustrations in this book were done in acrylic.

Candlewick Press
2067 Massachusetts Avenue
Cambridge, Massachusetts 02140

visit us at www.candlewick.com